Here Is
Big
Bunny

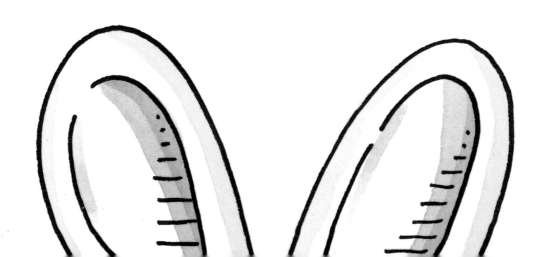

ALSO BY **Steve Henry**

Happy Cat

★"Successfully tells a simple tale and creates a sense of community using just 20 unique words. . . . Plenty of visual cues, lots of repetition and a clear story arc make this a perfect choice for beginning readers."
—*Kirkus Reviews*, starred review

Cat Got a Lot

"Another ideal story for newly hatched readers."
—*Kirkus Reviews*

Here Is
Big
Bunny

Steve Henry

Holiday House / New York

For Mary, my very first friend

HOLIDAY HOUSE is registered in the U.S. Patent and Trademark Office.
Printed and Bound in October 2015 at Tien Wah Press, Johor Bahru, Johor, Malaysia.
The artwork was drawn in ink and painted with watercolor, gouache and
acrylic paints on hot pressed watercolor paper.
www.holidayhouse.com
First Edition
1 3 5 7 9 10 8 6 4 2

Library of Congress Cataloging-in-Publication Data
Henry, Steve, 1948-
Here is Big Bunny / Steve Henry. — First edition.
pages cm.
Summary: Baffling sightings in a busy city—an ear behind a tall building, a nose outside a fancy store, a bushy tail in the park,
a foot outside the museum, and more—provide clues to the true identity of Big Bunny.
ISBN 978-0-8234-3458-9 (hardcover)
[1. Rabbits—Fiction. 2. Size—Fiction.] I. Title.
PZ7.H39732He 2016
[E]—dc23
2014048571

Here is a foot.

Here is a foot.

Here is a hand.

Here is a hand.

Here is a tail.

Here is a tail.

Here is an ear.

Here is an ear.

Here are ears.

Here is an eye.

Here is an eye.

Here is a nose.

Here is a nose.

Here is a face.

Here is a face.

Here is Big Bunny.

Here is Big Bunny.

Notes and Acknowledgments

Visiting a class of kindergarteners, I was thrilled by how deeply they "read" the pictures in my book *Happy Cat*. In *Happy Cat*, cutaways of an apartment building show a cat walking up stairs from one floor to the next. At the top of the illustrations, readers can see just the feet of the animals on the next floor. The kindergarteners loved guessing what those animals might be. They really wanted to turn the page to find out who was there. I was elated by their excitement, as well as impressed by their visual literacy.

I asked the kindergarteners what animal they would like me to write about and to draw in my next book. They answered, "Cats!" "Dogs!" "Monkeys!" "Horses!" A boy sitting on the floor at the edge of the group raised his hand and said, "What if you draw the biggest bunny in the world?" That idea intrigued me and stayed with me. I later made a quick drawing of a big bunny and taped it to the inside of my apartment door. I saw it every time I went out.

Growing up, I loved the drawings of Hilary Knight and Garth Williams: Hilary Knight for his building cutaways, playful and plentiful details and his bird's eye perspectives; Garth Williams for his city scenes, his interiors and his animals. *Here Is Big Bunny* has more than one hundred fifty animal characters, not counting Big Bunny himself. Also, I have always admired Charles Schultz for his ability to show all ranges of expression with a simple line, as well as the Warner Brothers and Disney cartoonists.

"Henri Matisse: The Cut-Outs" was at the Museum of Modern Art while I was working on the drawings for *Here Is Big Bunny*, and of course, Matisse inspired a piece of art in the illustration of the museum, as did the art of Henry Moore, Pablo Picasso and Alexander Calder.

After three years, much thought and many sketches . . . Here Is Big Bunny. I am grateful to all mentioned above for helping me deliver him to you.

And thank-you to my editor Grace Maccarone. It was with her smart and patient help that I moved my Big Bunny down the street. Her history of the doing the same with a Big Red Dog made all work go smoothly. And it was fun!

Steve Henry